"The Lion King: Roar" is based on the original story
The Lion King: Roar, illustrated by Adam Devancy and Darren Hont.
"The Little Mermaid: Ariel and the Very Best Book" is based on the original story
The Little Mermaid: Ariel and the Very Best Book, illustrated by Sol Studios.
"Lady and the Tramp: What's That Noise?" is based on the original story
Lady and the Tramp: What's That Noise?, illustrated by Sol Studios.
"Aladdin: Abu Monkeys Around" is based on the original story
Aladdin: Abu Monkeys Around, illustrated by Darren Hont.
"Toy Story: Buzz and the Bubble Planet" is based on the original story
Toy Story: Buzz and the Bubble Planet, illustrated by Sol Studios.

This is a Parragon book
This edition published in 2005

Printed in China
ISBN 1-40546-248-5

Easy-to-read Stories

THE
LION KING

by Patricia Grossman

The day begins.
Simba and Nala say hello.
Then they start to roar.

Simba roars at the tall giraffes.
The giraffes chew the grass.
They toss their heads.

Nala roars at the monkeys.
They are busy.
The monkeys just laugh
at Nala.

Simba roars at the
big elephants.
They are not afraid.
The elephants just
trumpet back.

Nala roars at the zebras.
The zebras do not look up.
They just keep eating.

Simba and Nala see Zazu.
Zazu is napping high in a tree.
Now Simba and Nala
can have some fun!

Simba roars at Zazu.
Simba's roar is loud!
Zazu keeps napping.
He does not hear Simba.

Nala roars at Zazu.
Nala's roar is loud!
Zazu does not hear Nala, either.
He just keeps dreaming.

Simba and Nala look
at each other.
Then they look at Zazu.
At last they *both* roar at Zazu.
Their roar is very loud!

Goodbye, nap.
Goodbye, dreams.
Goodbye, snores.
"Go and roar somewhere else!"
shouts Zazu.
Nala and Simba just laugh!

The End

Disney's THE LITTLE MERMAID

Ariel and the Very Best Book

by Patrick Daley and Joan Michael

"Where is Ariel?"
asked the King of the Sea.
Sebastian said,
"She is reading again.
Come with us
and you will see."

King Triton scolded Ariel.
"Why must you read
all day and all night?
Books are for people.
This just is not right."

"But, Father, I will show you
how great books can be.
I will show you my best books.
Then you will see."

"Look, Father, look.
Look at this book.
It has pictures and maps
and places to go.
There are wonderful places.
These are places to know."

King Triton frowned.
"A book full of maps?
That is no good to me.
I have no need for maps.
I live in the sea!"

Ariel tried again.
"Look at this book.
It is full of fish.
It tells all about them.
It tells all you wish."

"A book about fish?
That is no good to me.
I know all about fish,"
said the King of the Sea.

"I will find you a book,"
Ariel said with a smile.
"I will find a book.
But it may take a while."

"I will draw and I will write.
I will cut and I will colour.

I will make him a book
that is like no other."

Said the King of the Sea,
"What is this book
you are giving to me?
It tells all about
our life in the sea!
Yes, this is a good book.
I have to agree."

"It is the very best book,"
said the King of the Sea.
"Would you like to read it?
Would you read it to me?"

What's That Noise?

by Carol Pugliano-Martin

It was a dark night.
Lady and Tramp were alone
in the house.
Suddenly, Lady heard a noise.

"What's that noise?" Lady asked Tramp.
"The floor is making that noise,"
said Tramp.
Lady was not so sure.
But Tramp said,
"Lady, we are safe and sound.
I am the bravest dog around!"

Tramp shut his eyes.
But Lady could not sleep.
"I must watch the house!"
she said.

Then Lady heard another noise.
She shook Tramp.
"What's that noise?" Lady asked.

"That noise is just the wind," said Tramp.
"Lady, we are safe and sound. I am the bravest dog around!"

Lady heard another noise!
Bang! Crash!
Who was outside the house?

"What's that noise?"
Lady asked Tramp.
Tramp said,
"That is just thunder.
Lady, we are safe and sound.
I am the bravest dog around!"

"I hope you are right," Lady said.
Lady heard another sound.
Plink! Plink!
Was there someone *inside* the house?

Lady ran to the kitchen
and barked.
Tramp ran in.
"What's that noise?" Lady asked.
"That noise is the rain
falling into the pot," Tramp said.

"Lady, we are safe and sound.
I am the bravest dog around!"

Lady heard the windows shake.
Then she heard a loud bark.
"*Ruff! Ruff! Ruff!*"
It was Tramp!

Tramp was looking at
a big shadow on the wall.
"What is that?" Tramp asked Lady.
Lady had to find out what it was.

Lady said, "I must be brave."
She looked at the rug.
The big shadow was
a teeny, tiny bug!

Tramp was still on the piano.
"Do not be afraid," Lady said.
"It is a teeny, tiny bug."
"I was not afraid," Tramp said.

"Tramp, you were right," Lady said.
"We are safe and sound."
"That's right," Tramp said.
"We are the bravest dogs around!"

Aladdin

Abu Monkeys Around

by Anne Schreiber

From Monday,
when the week began,
to Sunday, at its end,
Abu played tricks on the Genie
and all of the Genie's friends.

On Monday,
everyone was sleeping.

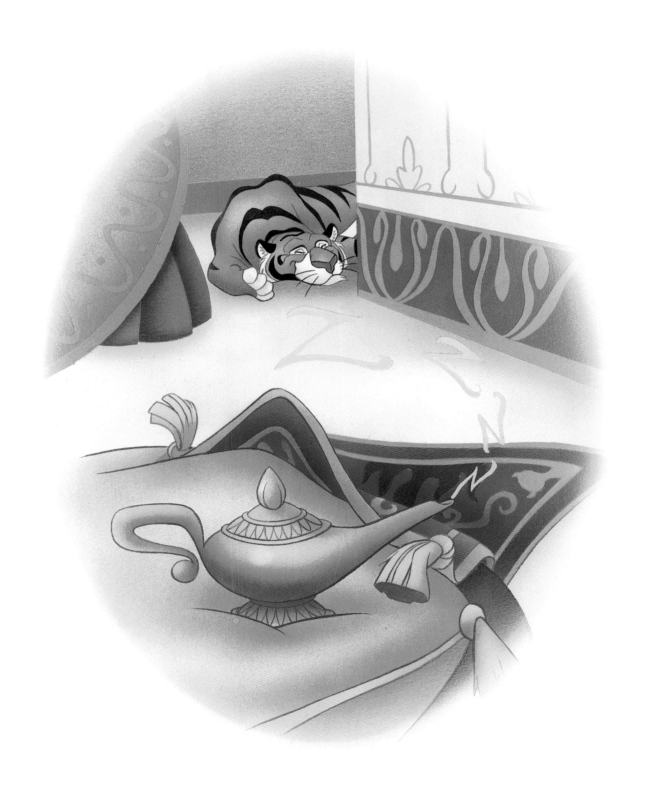

Except Abu.
Bang!

Abu banged the lamp.
It started to shake.
It fell on the floor.
Is the Genie awake?

On Tuesday,
the Genie was combing.

But not Abu.
Clang!

Abu scared the Genie
by ringing a bell.
The Genie jumped up.
Down Abu fell.

On Wednesday,
everyone was eating.

Except Abu.
Crash!

Abu spilled the juice.
He dropped the fruit.

The Genie got juice
all over his suit.

On Thursday,
everyone was resting.

Except Abu.
Splash!

Abu jumped into the water.
He wanted to swim.
Aladdin got wet.
The Genie fell in.

On Friday,
everyone went shopping.

Except Abu.
Whoosh!

Abu left a mess
on the ground.
His friends walked by
and slid all around.

On Saturday,
everyone was working.

Except Abu.
Swoosh!

Abu jumped up
to grab a sweet treat.
He knocked over a basket.
Apples rolled
down the street.

What has Abu done?

On Monday he woke the Genie.

On Tuesday he made things crash.

On Wednesday he spilled the juice.

On Thursday he made a splash.

On Friday he left a mess,
and all his friends fell down.

On Saturday he jumped on a fruit stall,
and spilled apples on the ground.

On Sunday, when
the week was through,
no one could sleep.

Except Abu!
Zzzzzzzzzzz.

BUZZ AND THE BUBBLE PLANET

by Judy Katschke

There was a new toy in Andy's room.
"It looks like a spaceship,"
said Woody.
"Did you say 'spaceship'?"
Buzz asked.

Buzz got in the spaceship.
Woody told Buzz to be careful.

Buzz was ready to blast off.
"Buzz, don't go!" Woody said.
Uh-oh!
Woody hit the 'on' switch.

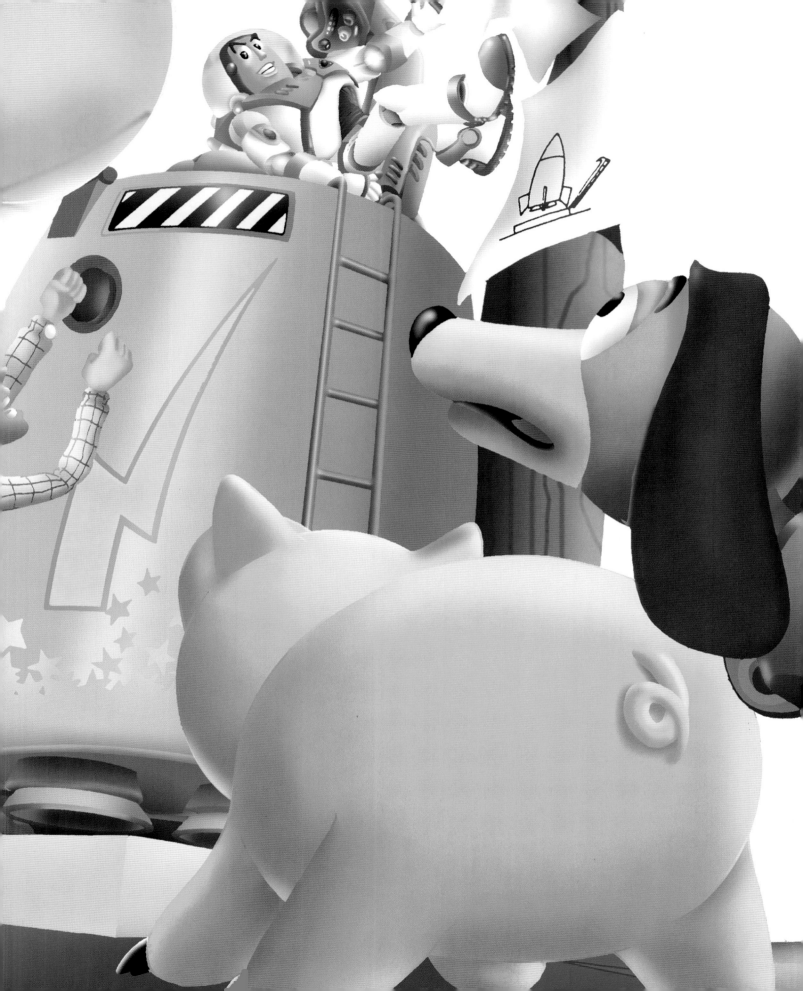

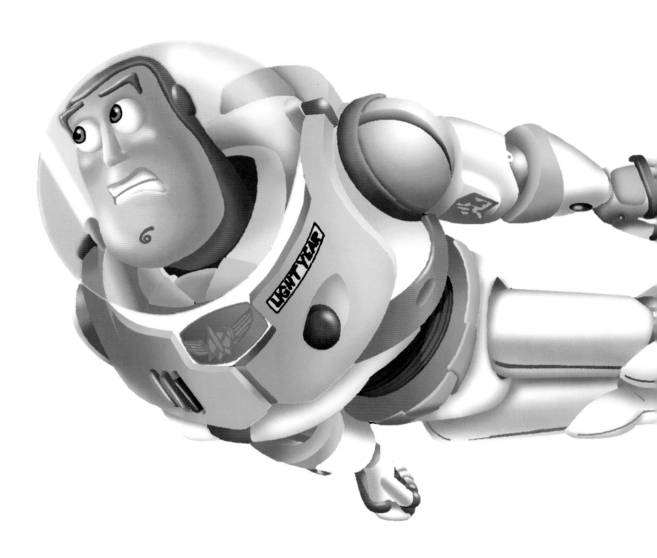

Whoosh!

The spaceship went
up, up, and away!
Then it came down.
Buzz fell out.

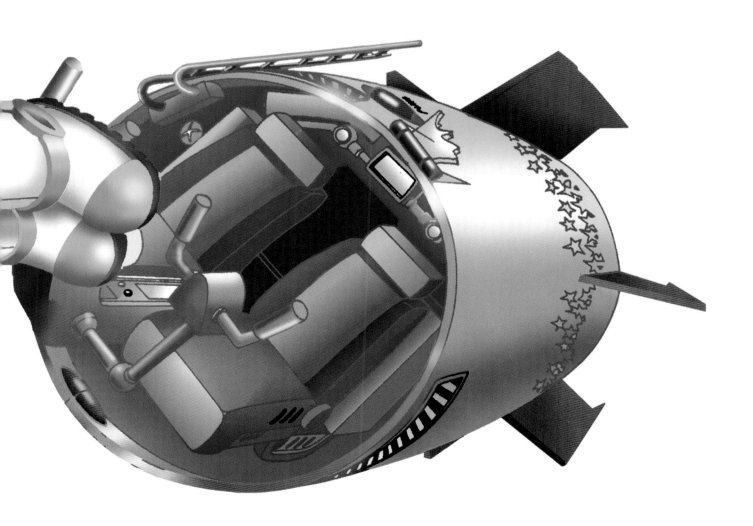

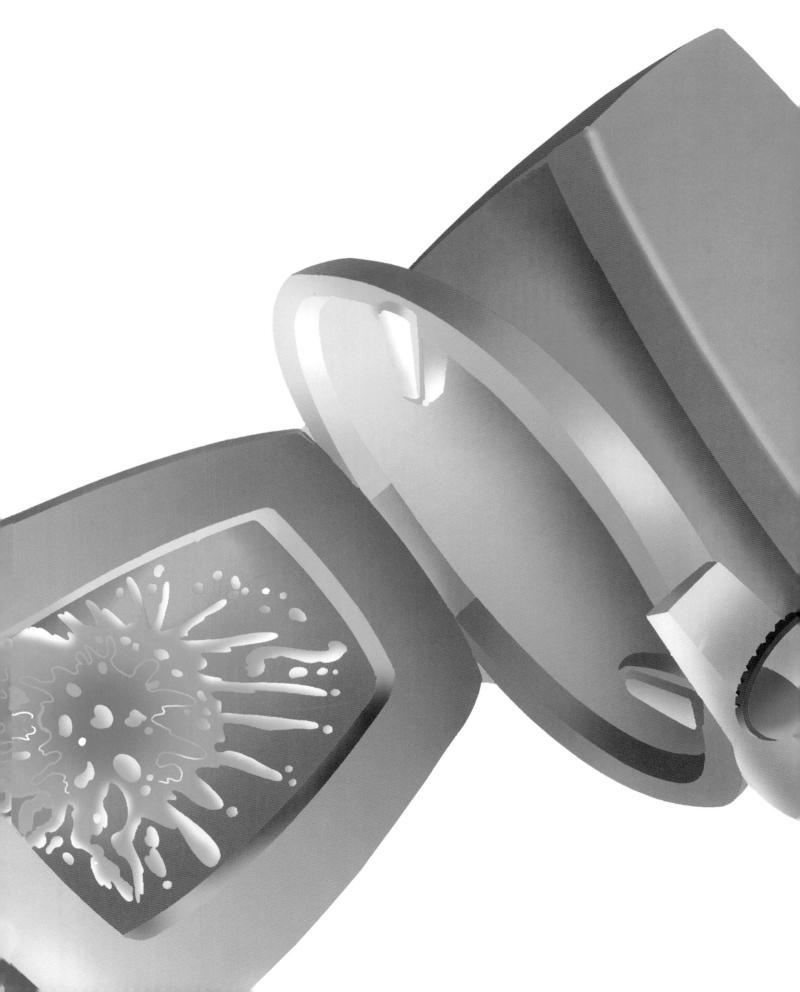

Buzz landed in some water.
He jumped out.
The water went down.

"I am on a strange planet,"
said Buzz.
"I must look around.
After all, I *am* Buzz Lightyear!
But how will I get home?"
he said.

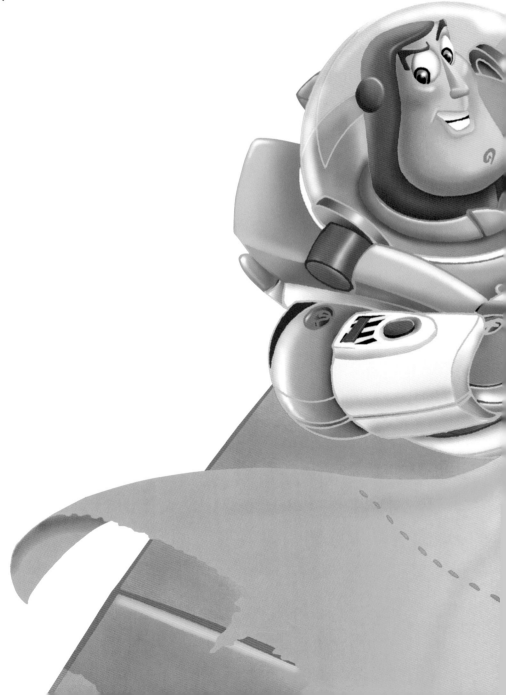

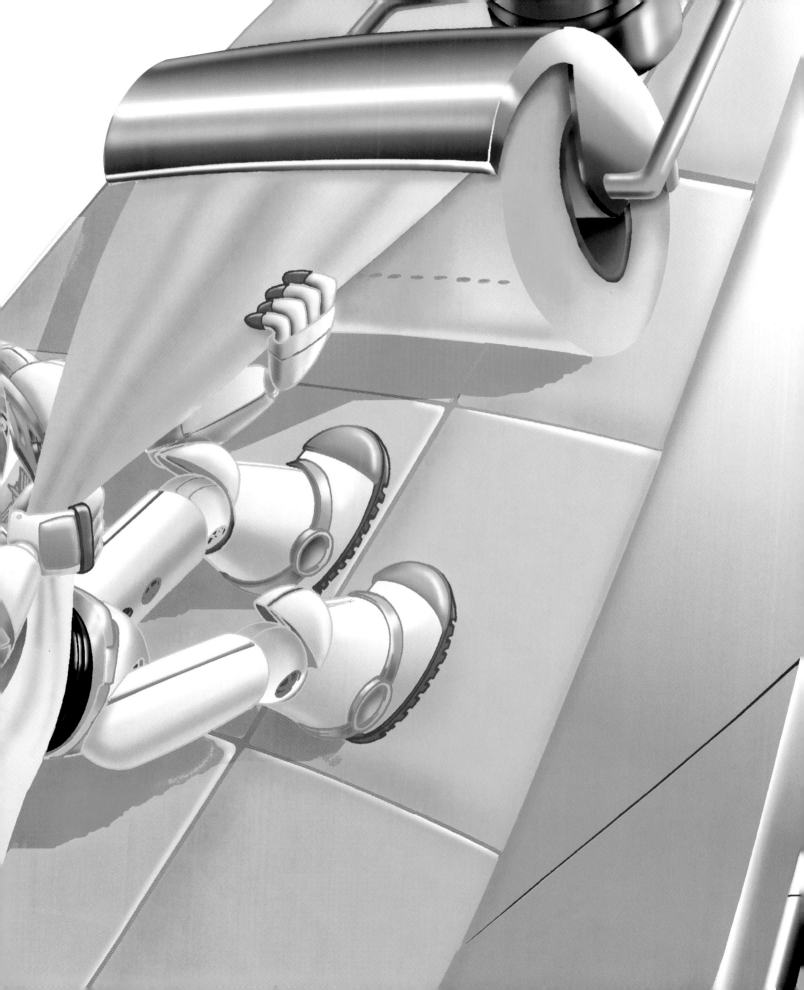

Back in Andy's room,
the toys held a meeting.
"We must find Buzz," said Woody.
"I will send out the green
army men," said Sarge.
"Great idea!" said the toys.

Buzz was in trouble.

A robot was pushing him.

It shook in his hands.

Buzz could not hold on.

Buzz hit a button.

The robot stopped.

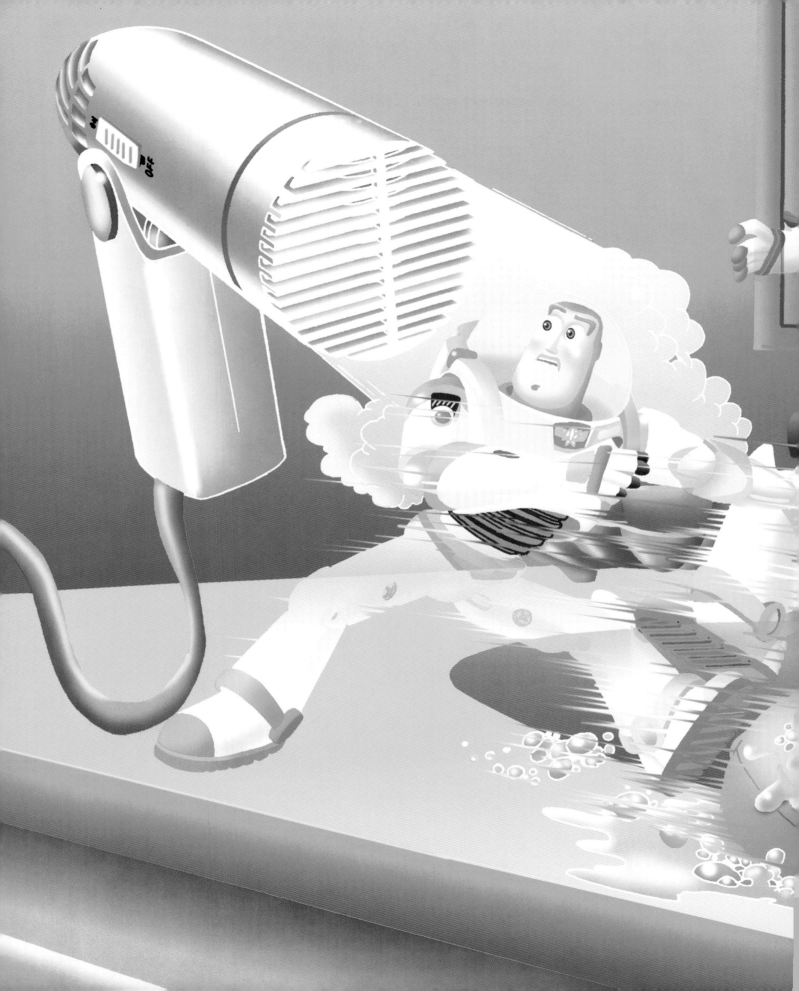

Next, strong winds
pushed Buzz.
He slipped on a rock.
He was covered in blue slime.

Buzz saw Andy's cat, Whiskers.
"Do not worry, Whiskers.
I will rescue you," said Buzz.
The cat's tail swung at Buzz.

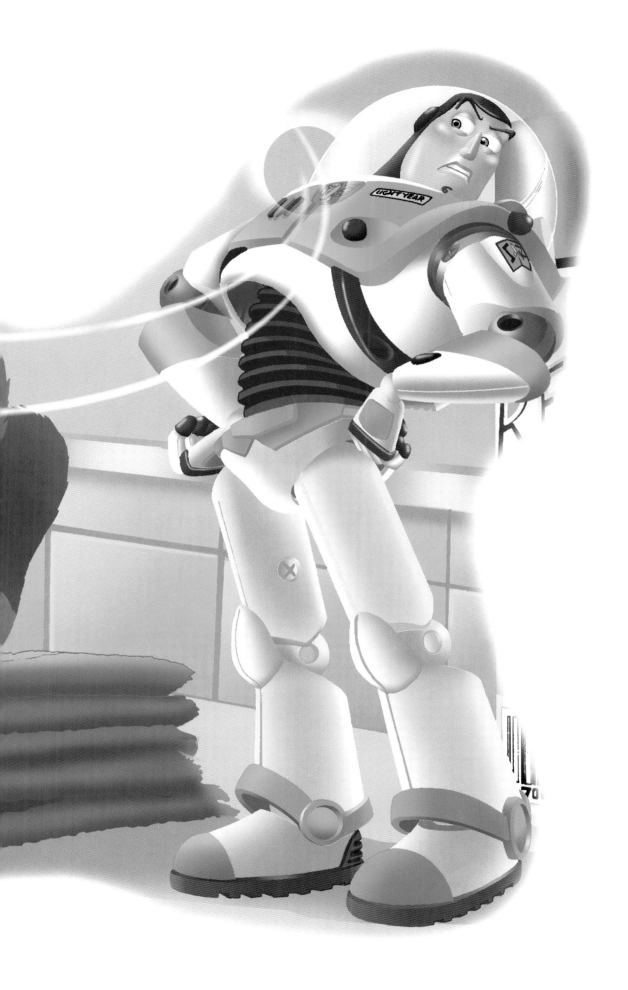

THUMP!
Buzz was in a red boat.
"This planet moves
too much," said Buzz.

Buzz saw yellow aliens.
They swam to him.
"Who is your leader?"
Buzz called.
"Squeak," said the yellow aliens.

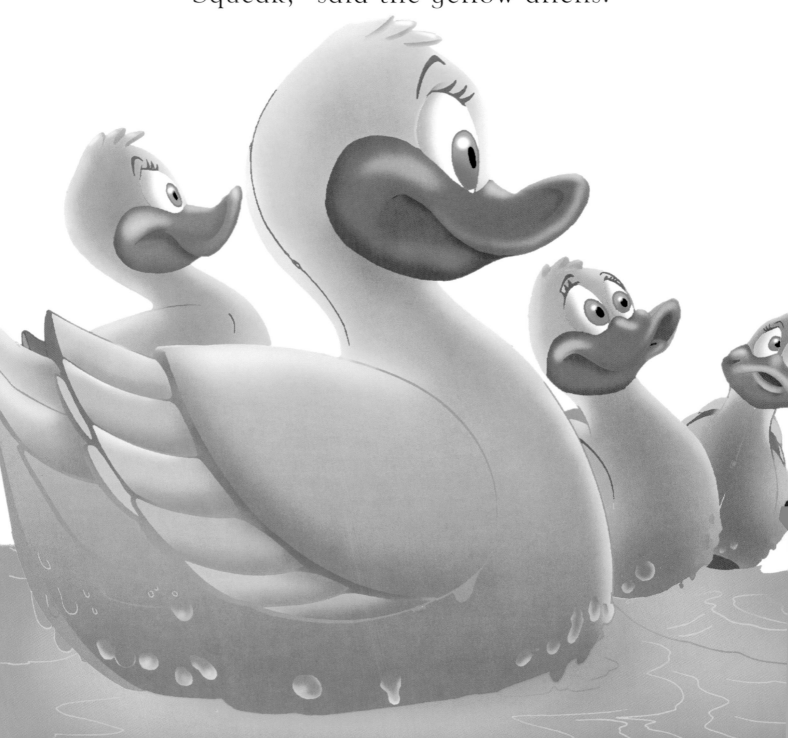

Buzz's wings opened.
His wings hit a bottle of
Squeakyclean
Bubbles.

"You must be Squeak,"
Buzz said.
"I am Buzz Lightyear.
I come in peace."

Thick pink goo
came out of Squeak's head.
The goo turned into lots of bubbles.
Buzz slapped the bubbles.
But they were all around him.

Sarge and his men saw Buzz.
Sarge called Woody.
"Should we save him?" he asked.

"Do not worry," said Woody.
"Help is on the way!"

Back on the Bubble Planet,
Buzz was in trouble again.
Aliens were all around him.
Soon he would fall
into Squeak's bubble trap.

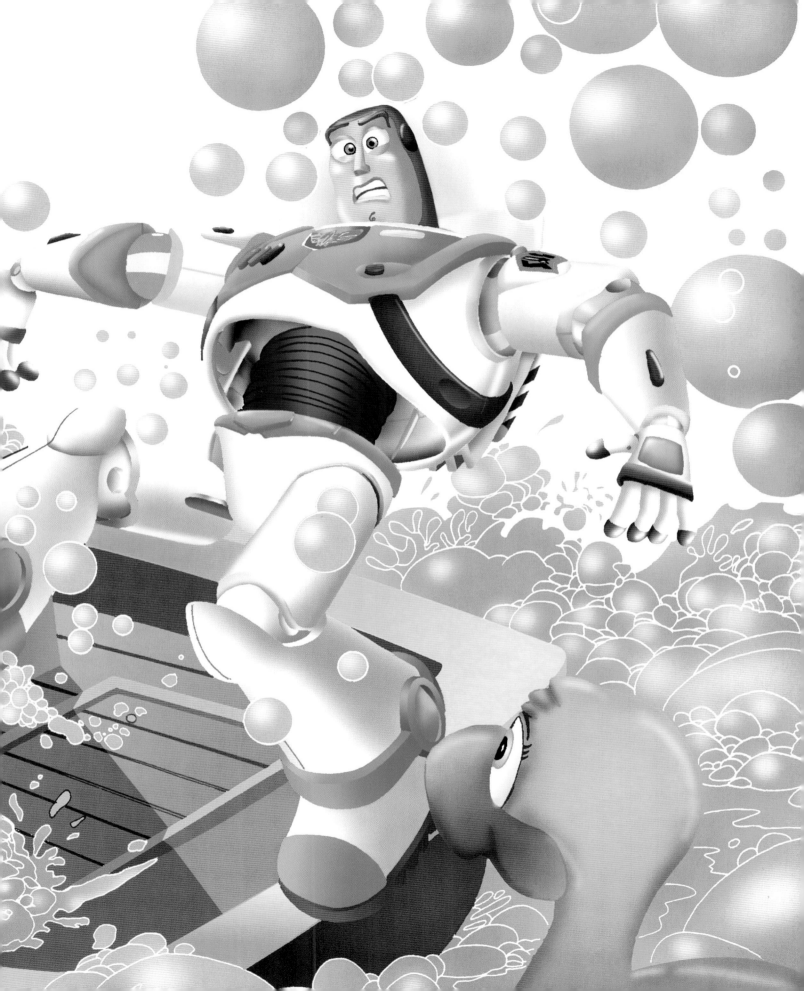

At last, help came.
Andy was on the Bubble Planet.
And Andy had Woody.
"Let's go, partners!"
Andy said.

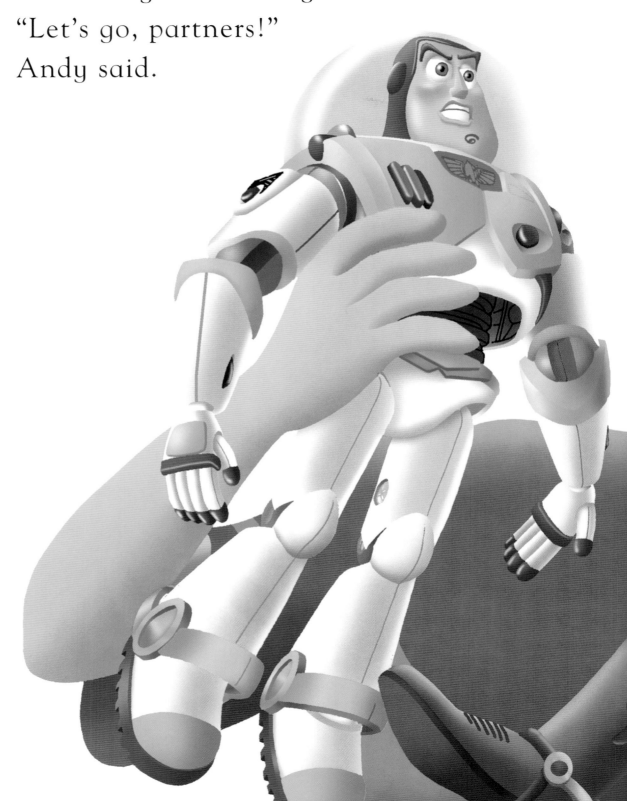

The Bubble Planet was
not so scary any more.
Buzz was happy.
His friends were here.
And he was clean!